ZACHARY
in
Camping Out

by Bertrand Gauthier
illustrations by Daniel Sylvestre

Gareth Stevens Publishing
MILWAUKEE

For a free color catalog describing Gareth Stevens's list of high-quality books, call 1-800-341-3569 (USA) or 1-800-461-9120 (Canada).

Library of Congress Cataloging-in-Publication Data

Gauthier, Bertrand.
  [Zunik dans la pleine lune. English]
  Zachary in Camping out / text by Bertrand Gauthier ; illustrated by Daniel Sylvestre.
    p. cm. — (Just me and my dad)
  Summary: Zachary and his dad camp at the seashore with friends at the time of the full moon.
    ISBN 0-8368-1012-0
    [1. Camping—Fiction. 2. Fathers and sons—Fiction. 3. Seashore—Fiction.]
  I. Sylvestre, Daniel, ill. II. Title. III. Title: Camping out. IV. Series.
  PZ7.G2343Zab   1993
  [E]—dc20   93-15457

This edition first published in 1993 by
Gareth Stevens Publishing
1555 North RiverCenter Drive, Suite 201
Milwaukee, Wisconsin 53212, USA

This edition first published in 1993 by Gareth Stevens, Inc. Original edition ©1989 by Les éditions la courte échelle inc., Montréal, under the title *Zunik dans la pleine lune*.

Series editor: Patricia Lantier-Sampon
Series designer: Karen Knutson

Printed in the United States of America
1 2 3 4 5 6 7 8 9 97 96 95 94 93

At this time, Gareth Stevens, Inc., does not use 100 percent recycled paper, although the paper used in our books does contain about 30 percent recycled fiber. This decision was made after a careful study of current recycling procedures revealed their dubious environmental benefits. We will continue to explore recycling options.

My father told me it would be a long drive,
but not *this* long.

The beach must be at the other end of the world. And that's a long way away.

Finally, we arrive. It was worth the long ride to the seashore.

At night, we sleep in a tent. Our campground is up in the mountains not far from the beach. I like camping out.

Sometimes, Andrea and I play with Zoe.
She's seven, and she lives right by the
beach. She's lucky; she lives by the sea
all year long.

After we go swimming, Zoe, Andrea, and I
start building a big castle.

Zoe tells us a story. She sure is good at stories. I listen to every word.

Zoe says that every time there is a full moon, a sea monster comes out of the ocean and walks around and scares everybody in sight.

The restaurant was great. Andrea and I drew pictures of our day on the beach on the paper placemats. Then, we went for a walk in the woods. I sure am tired now! Then, suddenly. . .

I'm trying to sleep, Zach. Don't be scared; the monster won't get you. Your Dad will protect you.
Who says I'm scared? How can I be scared of a monster that doesn't even exist?

I try as hard as I can to fall asleep, but there are too many sounds. The country is a lot noisier than the city. I'd rather hear cars than all these strange sounds in the night.

Finally, I fall asleep, but I have a bad dream.
There is a monster gobbling up David, Helen,
Andrea, Zoe, and. . .me.

Then, I wake up. The sun is shining. Whew,
no more full moon! That Zoe is a fibber!
There isn't any sea monster. And even if
there is one, my father will chase it away.

I love my father when he protects me
from monsters.